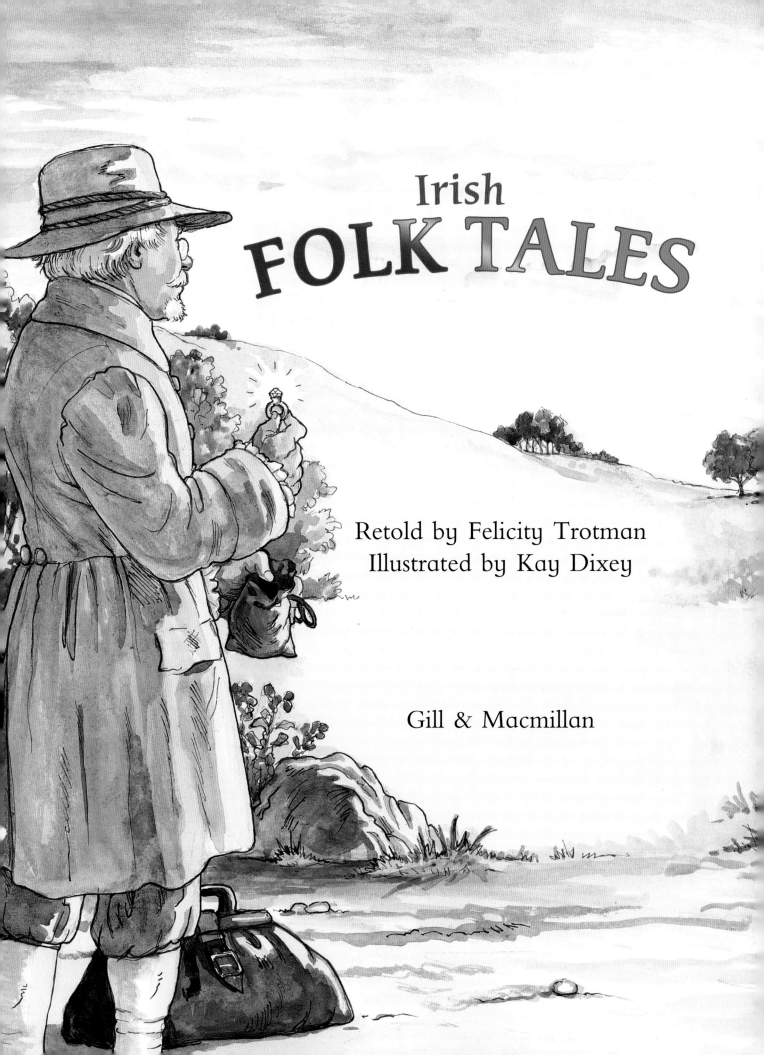

Irish
FOLK TALES

Retold by Felicity Trotman
Illustrated by Kay Dixey

Gill & Macmillan

CONTENTS

INTRODUCTION

This enchanting collection of six Irish folk tales features a captivating range of fairy characters. Discover how lazy Annie ensures she has a life of ease with the help of three elderly fairies. Share the doctor's delight when his care of a beautiful young woman and her baby makes him a wealthy man. Listen entranced as Felix O'Driscoll learns to believe in the little people and then there's Jack Dogherty who makes friends with a merrow.

The enduring appeal of Irish folk tales is enhanced by the lively illustrations in this entertaining compilation.

SEEING IS BELIEVING

Felix O'Driscoll was a noisy young man, who loved to swagger about and joke with his friends. He often boasted that he didn't believe in fairies, ghosts and cluricaunes. Nonetheless, he did sometimes feel a little nervous at night and when he rode past the old churchyard after dark, he always made his horse trot quickly and cast anxious looks all around him.

Most evenings, Felix and
his friends met in the village pub.
They loved sitting down together and
telling stories of fairy folk – each one tried
to outdo the others' stories!

Felix would laugh at these tales and always
insisted loudly that fairies didn't exist.
Although his friends might not have seen
any of the little people, they couldn't
quite bring themselves to say they
didn't believe in them.

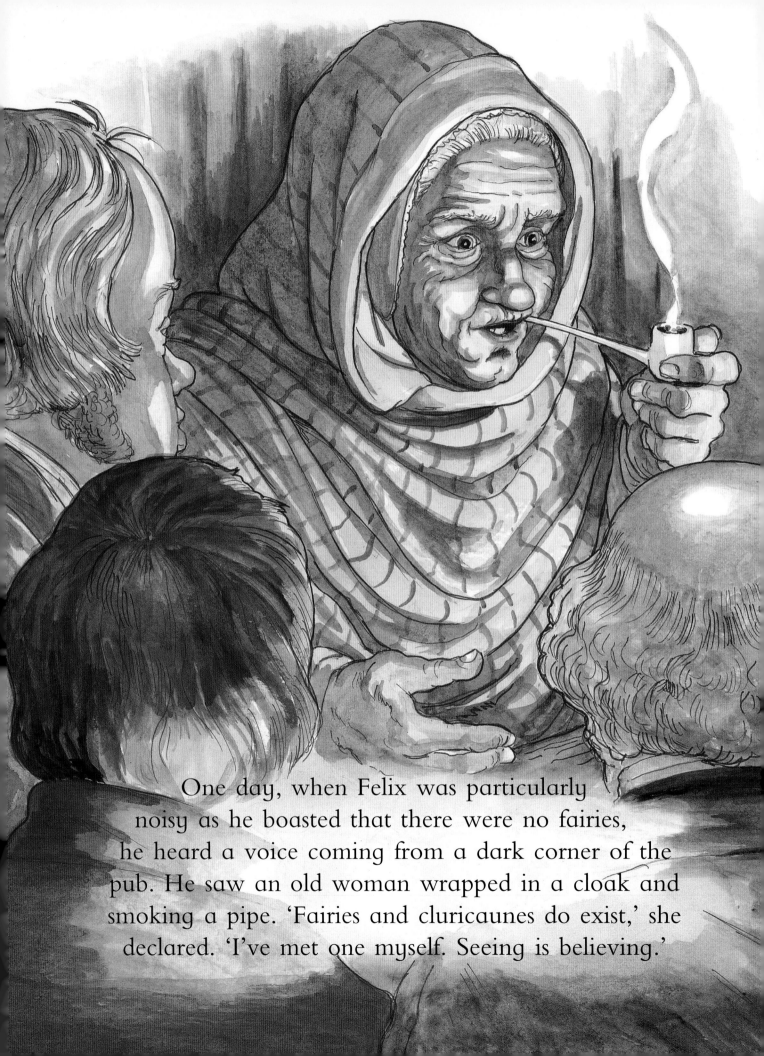

One day, when Felix was particularly
noisy as he boasted that there were no fairies,
he heard a voice coming from a dark corner of the
pub. He saw an old woman wrapped in a cloak and
smoking a pipe. 'Fairies and cluricaunes do exist,' she
declared. 'I've met one myself. Seeing is believing.'

Felix and his friends were intrigued. They gathered round the old woman. 'Tell us what happened,' they said to her.

'It was a very long time ago and I was still a young girl,' began the old woman. 'It was a lovely warm June day, and I was knitting in my garden, listening to the singing of the birds and watching butterflies fluttering from flower to flower. The air was fresh and sweet.

'I was keeping an eye on the bees, for they were about to swarm and were humming loudly as they flew from hive to hive.

'Suddenly I heard a noise! It was coming from the rows of beans in the corner of the garden, and it was a kind of tapping – tick-tack, tick-tack – just like a cobbler nailing the heel on a shoe.

'I put down my knitting, and crept quietly up to the beans. There in the middle was a tiny old man. He was wearing a black hat on his head, and a grey coat with big buttons. His shoes had silver buckles that were so large they almost covered his feet! He was smoking a little pipe and hammering the heels onto a pair of shoes. I knew at once that he was a cluricaune.'

9

'"Good day to you," I said. "That's hot work on a warm day."

'He looked up at me crossly. I reached down and grabbed him. When I had him in my hand, I asked him for his purse of gold.'

'"Gold?" he said. "And where would a poor old man like me get any money?"

'"None of your tricks!" I told him. "Everyone knows that each cluricaune has a magic purse – and that however often you take a coin out, there's always another coin left in the purse."

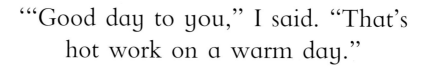

'I pulled a knife out of my pocket, and made the fiercest face I could at him. "Show me your purse of gold, or I'll cut the nose off your face!" I ordered.

'The little old man looked so frightened that I nearly let him go. "All right," he said, "you'll have to come with me a couple of fields away, and I'll show you where my money is."

11

'We set off towards the field. I held him firmly in my hand, and didn't take my eyes off him. Suddenly I heard a loud buzzing just behind me. "Watch out!" the cluricaune shouted. "Your bees are swarming!"

'I turned my head, fool that I was, but saw nothing at all. Then I looked back at the cluricaune in my hand – but my hand was empty! I had taken my eyes off him, and he had disappeared like smoke. He never came near my garden again.'

The old woman sat back when she finished her story. Felix and his friends looked at each other in amazement – but it seemed as if the story must be true.

Felix certainly believed her – and never again did anyone hear him say that he didn't believe in the little people!

THE DOCTOR AND THE FAIRY PRINCESS

It was late at night and there was a knock at the doctor's door. When he opened it, he saw a big black coach drawn by black horses.

There was a small boy on the front step. 'Please speak to my master,' the boy said. The doctor put his head through the window of the coach.

14

'Could you come at once?
My wife needs you urgently,'
asked the man inside.

'I'll be with you in five minutes,' the doctor
said. He dressed as quickly as possible, snatched
up his bag, and joined the fine gentleman in the
coach. 'Sit beside me,' said the gentleman, 'and
don't be alarmed at anything you may see.'

The coach moved at great speed, heading for Lough Neagh. When they got to the jetty, the doctor thought they would slow down to get on the ferry – but the coach didn't stop!

It sped right through the water, across the lough! The doctor began to feel nervous, as he realised what sort of a patient he had been called to help.

Soon the coach reached the far bank of Lough Neagh.
The horses did not stop galloping as their hooves hit
dry ground. At last the carriage came to a halt and
the doctor climbed out in front of a large house.

The gentleman waved at an open door. The doctor
was led down a corridor and into a well-lit room
hung with bright silk, embroidered in gold and silver.
A fire roared in the hearth.

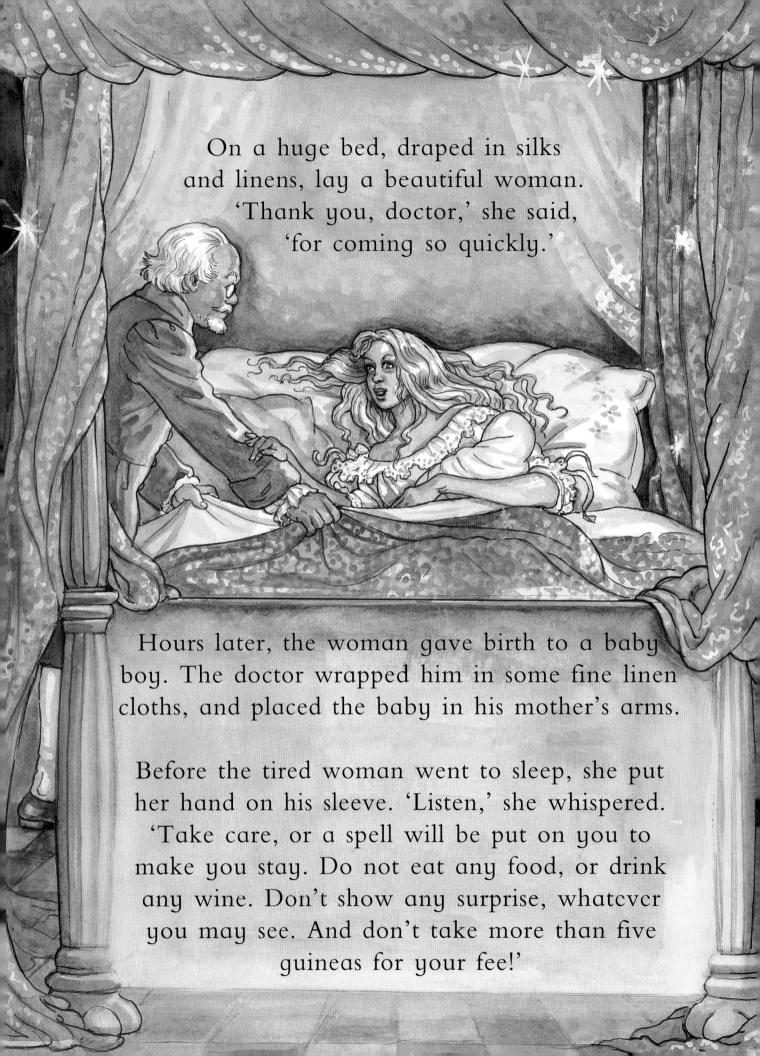

On a huge bed, draped in silks
and linens, lay a beautiful woman.
'Thank you, doctor,' she said,
'for coming so quickly.'

Hours later, the woman gave birth to a baby
boy. The doctor wrapped him in some fine linen
cloths, and placed the baby in his mother's arms.

Before the tired woman went to sleep, she put
her hand on his sleeve. 'Listen,' she whispered.
'Take care, or a spell will be put on you to
make you stay. Do not eat any food, or drink
any wine. Don't show any surprise, whatever
you may see. And don't take more than five
guineas for your fee!'

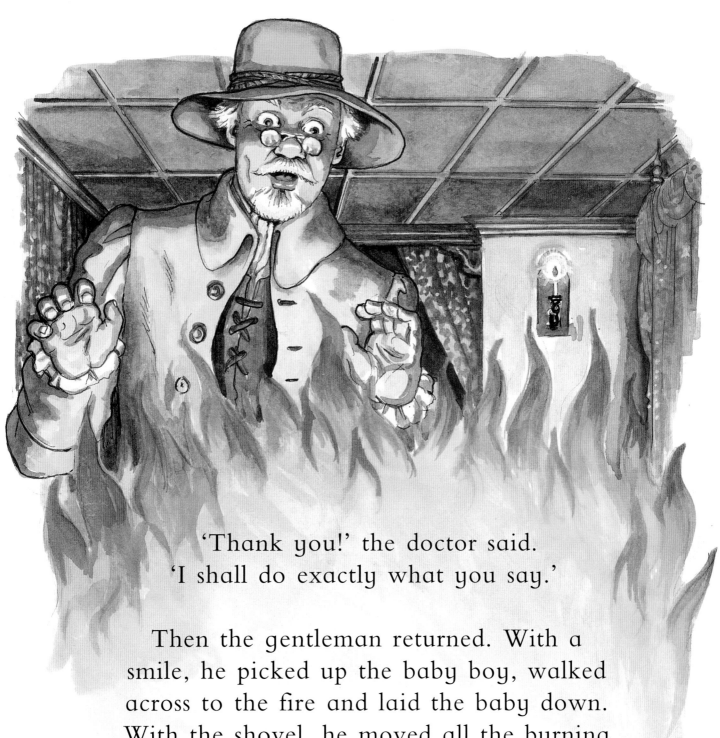

'Thank you!' the doctor said.
'I shall do exactly what you say.'

Then the gentleman returned. With a
smile, he picked up the baby boy, walked
across to the fire and laid the baby down.
With the shovel, he moved all the burning
coal to the front of the hearth and put the
baby on the hot stone at the back of the
fire. Then he covered the baby completely
with the hot coal! The doctor watched in
horror but he did not make a sound.

The next moment the doctor
found himself in a great hall.
A wonderful feast was laid
and many people were sitting
down, preparing to eat.

'You must be tired and hungry,'
said the gentleman. 'Please join
our feast.' The doctor remembered
his instructions. 'Sir,' he said,
'I never eat or drink between
supper and breakfast. Please let
me go home. Other patients
will be waiting for me.'

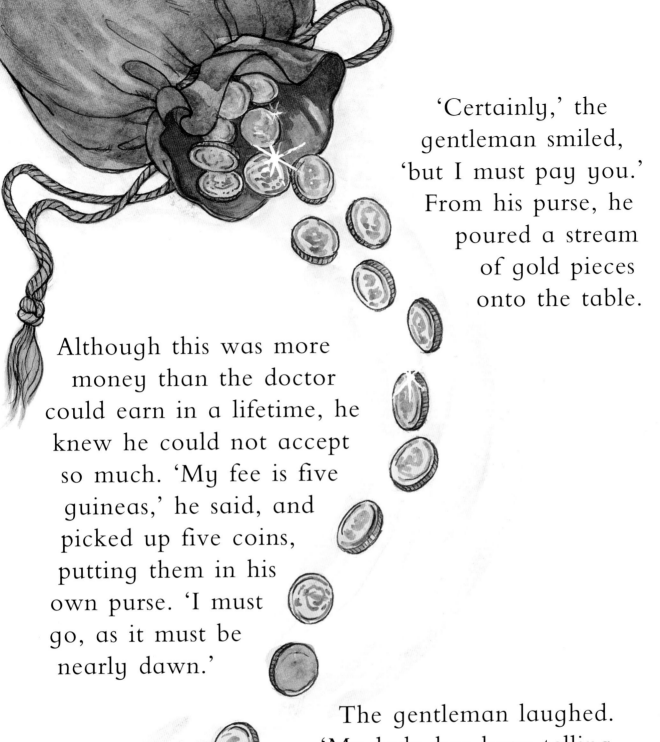

'Certainly,' the gentleman smiled, 'but I must pay you.' From his purse, he poured a stream of gold pieces onto the table.

Although this was more money than the doctor could earn in a lifetime, he knew he could not accept so much. 'My fee is five guineas,' he said, and picked up five coins, putting them in his own purse. 'I must go, as it must be nearly dawn.'

The gentleman laughed. 'My lady has been telling you secrets!' he said. 'You have done well. The coach is waiting for you, and will take you home safely.'

Once again, the doctor journeyed rapidly across the land and through the water. At last the carriage drew up outside his own front door and there the doctor climbed out.

When he pulled out his purse, he found a gold ring set with a huge diamond there too. His own name had been engraved inside the ring. He watched as the coach drove towards the rising sun.

The doctor realised that the ring was a reward from the fine gentleman himself – the fairy prince. From that day on, the fairy's gift brought him and his family all the luck, honour and riches that they could possibly want.

23

SOUL CAGES

One day Jack Dogherty met a merrow. He was wearing a red cocked hat, and was on the end of the rocks near Jack's home. Jack crossed the rocks carefully, not wanting to scare the sea fairy away. 'Good day to you, Jack,' the merrow said to him. 'How do you know my name?' asked Jack, astonished.

'Your grandfather was a great friend of mine,' the merrow told him. 'We often used to enjoy a drink together. So of course I know who you are!'

'Where do you get drink under the sea?' asked Jack. 'I thought it was all salt water.' 'There are barrels and bottles in ships that sink,' the merrow said. 'Why don't you come and try some? Meet me here tomorrow, and I'll take you to my house!'

25

Jack quickly agreed, and the next day he went out to the rocks again.

The merrow was there, holding two red hats. 'I've borrowed one for you,' he explained. 'Put this on, jump in and hold my tail.' Putting on his own hat, the merrow dived into the sea. Jack put on the other hat, jumped in, and grasped the merrow's tail.

Down they went through the water,
until they got to a flat, dry, sandy area.
There were fishes swimming overhead, and
seaweed rose up like trees. In front of them
was a pretty cottage, with smoke
coming out of the chimney.
Inside, a splendid meal of
fish was waiting for them.

Over dinner, washed down with
delicious things out of the merrow's
enormous collection of bottles, Jack learned
that the merrow's name was Coomara, but
usually he was called Coo. They talked and
laughed for hours, as friends do.

One thing puzzled Jack. There were rows of wicker cages like lobster pots stacked against the walls. 'What do you keep in those?' he asked at last.

'Oh, those are soul cages,' Coo told him. 'I put them out when there's a storm at sea. The souls of drowned fishermen and sailors creep into them, and then I bring them back here to keep them where it's warm and dry.'

Jack peered into a couple of cages
near him. He couldn't see anything,
but he could hear the sound of crying.

He felt very sorry for the souls, shut in
cages when they should be on their
way to Heaven. What could he do?

When the time came to go home, he thanked Coo very much for his great evening, and arranged to meet him out on the rocks the next day.

Back home, Jack thought hard about what he could do for the trapped souls. At last he worked out a plan. Next day, he invited Coo to come to his house.

Like the merrow, Jack collected bottles that were washed up on the beach after storms and shipwrecks. That evening, when Coo came, Jack had built up a good fire, so the cabin was beautifully warm.

He produced some bottles of very old, strong brandy. Coo drank a glass while Jack only sipped at his. He poured Coo another, but soon the old merrow fell asleep by the fire.

Quickly, Jack took Coo's red
hat. He ran to the rocks,
jammed the hat on his head,
and leapt into the sea.
In a flash, he came
to Coo's house.

As fast as
he could, he
collected all the
soul cages, and took
them outside. He opened
each one and shook it.
There was a tiny flicker from each cage, and
a faint whistle. When every one was empty,
Jack carried them inside and stacked them
where he'd found them.

When he got back to his home, Coo was still sleeping by the fire. When he woke, he thanked Jack and went off. To Jack's surprise, Coo never noticed that his soul cages had been emptied! The two remained friends for years, though every time there was a storm Jack would slip down to rescue any souls that Coo had trapped in his soul cages.

PAYING THE RENT

Bill Doody was sitting on a rock by a beautiful lake in Killarney. It was early one lovely May morning but Bill wasn't enjoying the view over the sunlit water or listening to the birdsong. He was in despair as he thought about his wife and his four little children. 'Tomorrow the rent is due, and I haven't

any money,' he said to himself. 'What are we going to do? And where will we go? If I can't pay the rent, our goods will be taken and we'll all be thrown out of our house to starve.' He had seen no one around, so he got quite a fright when a tall, well-built man suddenly appeared from a clump of gorse growing by the lake's edge.

'What's the matter with you?' the man asked Bill.

Who could this man be? thought Bill. Where had he come from? Was he even from this world? But he plucked up his courage to answer the man.

'My cows have given no milk, so I have no butter to sell, and if I can't pay my rent by midday tomorrow, I am going to be turned out of my farm. And then what will happen to my wife and children? I don't know what to do.'

'That's a sad story,' said the big man. 'But if you tell it to your landlord, surely he'll not be so cruel as to turn you out?' 'You don't know my landlord!' Bill told him. 'He's a hard man – and anyway, he's had his eye on my farm for a long time. He wants to give it to one of his relatives, so I know he'll do nothing to help us.'

Bill's hat was lying on
the ground beside him.
The stranger pulled a fat purse
from his pocket, opened it
and poured a stream of
gold into the hat.

'Take this!'
he said. 'Pay
your rent, but it won't
do your landlord any good.
I remember better times, when
I would have dealt severely with
someone as greedy and
unkind as that!'

Bill stared
at the gold in
amazement. Then he
tried to bless the man and
thank him but he had gone.

Bill saw him far away, riding a
handsome white horse across the
lake. Suddenly, he realised who it
was. 'O'Donoghue!' shouted Bill. 'It
was the great prince O'Donoghue!'
Bill knew all the stories about this
ancient prince. He had been a wise
and just ruler and then he had gone
to live in a palace in Tír na nÓg.
Sometimes he came back from under
the waters of the lake to help lost
travellers and poor people.

Bill raced home to tell his wife Judy what had happened, and show her the gold. She couldn't believe that suddenly their luck seemed to be changing. The next day, Bill went straight to his landlord's house. 'Hand over your rent, Doody,' the landlord snarled. 'And if it's a penny short, you'll be out on your ear before nightfall!' 'Here you are,' said Bill. 'Please count it, and give me a receipt.'

The landlord was expecting to see piles of copper coins on his desk – or maybe a few small silver ones, or a grubby banknote. He was stunned to see gold pieces! Quickly, he counted the money – it was the exact amount.

The landlord was furious that Bill had paid up, and he had not been able to ruin him. Without speaking, he wrote out a receipt and pushed it into Bill's hand. Then he showed Bill the door and returned to his desk.

To his astonishment, instead
of gold he saw a pile of gingerbread
cakes! Each one had the king's head
stamped on it, just like a coin. He raged and
swore — but he had given Bill a receipt for his
rent, so there was nothing he could do. Everyone
would laugh at him if people heard the story
of how Bill had got the better of him.

From that day on Bill Doody grew
rich, and he and his family often blessed
the day he met the great O'Donoghue.

LAZY ANNIE AND HER AMAZING AUNTS

Annie was very beautiful.
She was also the laziest girl in Ireland! One day
a prince rode by. 'Surely you aren't scolding that lovely girl?'
he asked when he heard her mother giving out. The old
woman was ashamed to admit how lazy Annie was.

44

She said, 'My daughter works too hard! She can spin, weave and make the cloth into shirts within three days.'

'My mother is the best spinner in the kingdom,' said the prince. 'I'd like to take Annie home with me and introduce her to the queen!'

The old woman didn't want to admit she had been untruthful about Annie's skill at spinning and weaving, so she agreed that her daughter should go. Annie was delighted to be invited to the prince's home. She sat on his horse, and they rode away together.

On the journey, Annie and the prince fell in love. They planned to marry – but Annie didn't dare confess that she couldn't spin, or weave, or sew! What was she to do?

When they reached the castle, the queen welcomed Annie. She could see how beautiful Annie was but she was even more pleased to hear that she was such a hard worker.

That night, Annie found a huge pile of flax on her bedroom floor. 'Start first thing in the morning,' the queen told her. 'I'll look forward to seeing the thread the day after tomorrow. Goodnight!'

The next morning, Annie started to cry because she couldn't spin. Suddenly, a funny old woman with very big feet appeared! 'Why are you crying?' she asked Annie. 'I have to spin all this by tomorrow, and I don't know how to do it,' Annie sobbed. 'Leave it to me,' the old woman said. 'Ask Colliach Cushmor to your wedding, and the thread will be ready tomorrow.' 'Of course I'll invite you,' Annie said. 'You'll be very welcome.'

By morning all
the flax had been
spun into the finest thread.
The queen was delighted.
'Excellent!' she said.
'Tomorrow you can weave
that into cloth on my own
loom. Have it done by evening.'
Annie was very frightened.
She had no idea how to use
a loom! She was sitting beside
it sobbing when an old woman
with huge hips appeared.
'I'm Colliach Cromanmor,'
she announced. 'Invite
me to your wedding,
and I'll weave that
thread by tonight!'
'Please come!' Annie
said. And so the
old woman
started work.

That evening, the queen ran the cloth through her hands. 'How soft and delicate!' she exclaimed. 'Make it into shirts tomorrow and my son will wear one at your wedding!'

Bright and early next morning, Annie sat sorrowfully by the cloth. She feared she would lose her prince, for she had no idea how to sew! It was midday when a third old woman arrived.

She had an enormous red nose! She introduced herself as Colliach Shron Mor Rua, and asked for a wedding invitation. 'I'd be delighted if you came,' Annie told her. By nightfall, the old woman had made twelve perfect shirts.

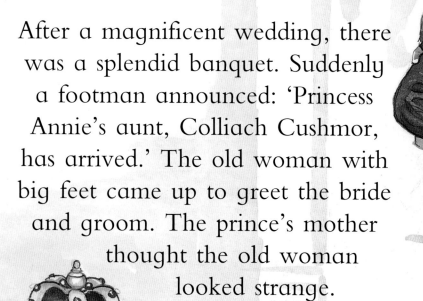

After a magnificent wedding, there was a splendid banquet. Suddenly a footman announced: 'Princess Annie's aunt, Colliach Cushmor, has arrived.' The old woman with big feet came up to greet the bride and groom. The prince's mother thought the old woman looked strange.

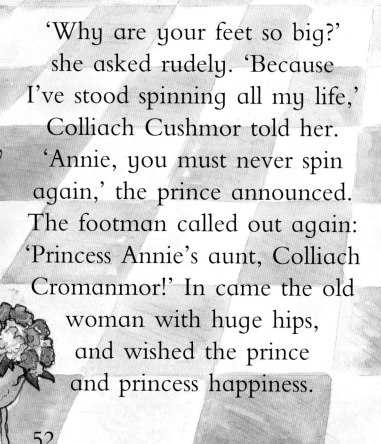

'Why are your feet so big?' she asked rudely. 'Because I've stood spinning all my life,' Colliach Cushmor told her. 'Annie, you must never spin again,' the prince announced. The footman called out again: 'Princess Annie's aunt, Colliach Cromanmor!' In came the old woman with huge hips, and wished the prince and princess happiness.

The queen stared. 'Why are your hips so huge?' she demanded. 'Because I've sat at a loom all my life,' the old woman answered. 'Darling, you must never weave again,' the prince told Annie. Again the footman called: 'Princess Annie's aunt, Colliach Shron Mor Rua!' The old woman with the red nose approached. 'Why is your nose red?' demanded the queen. 'Bent over my sewing every day, all my blood ran into my nose,' the old woman replied. 'Dearest, never sew!' cried the prince.

So, thanks to these three old fairies, Annie knew she need never spin, or weave, or sew, but could live for ever as an idle princess!

PADDY AND THE PHOUKA

Paddy loved stories about the fairy folk! He especially enjoyed stories about phoukas, who played jokes on people. They could be fierce and frightening, or kind and helpful.

One day, while looking after his father's cows, Paddy felt a strange wind, and knew it was a phouka, going to where the fairies danced. 'Phouka', he called out. 'Let me see you! You can have my coat to keep warm!'

Suddenly a big young bull charged at Paddy! He threw his coat on the animal. The bull stopped and said in a man's voice, 'Go to the mill tonight when the moon is full, and you'll have good luck!'

That night, Paddy went to the mill. There were sacks of corn lying around, but the men who worked there were asleep.

It was so late that Paddy was tired and went to sleep too – and when he woke in the morning, the corn had all been ground into flour. This was very strange, because all the men were still sleeping soundly.

For several nights the same thing happened. Paddy decided he must stay awake and see how the corn was ground!

So he crept
into an old chest
that he found in the mill.
The chest had a big keyhole,
and he could peep out of it.

That night, looking through the keyhole, he spied six little men coming in, each carrying a sack of corn on his back. They were followed by an old man, wearing torn and ragged clothes. The old man set the little people to work, and soon all the corn was ground. Paddy knew the old man was the phouka he had met, with six little phoukas.

In the morning, Paddy told
his father what he had seen.
'If the phouka wants
to work, I won't stop
him,' his father said,
'but I will sack the
lazy men who have
done nothing.'

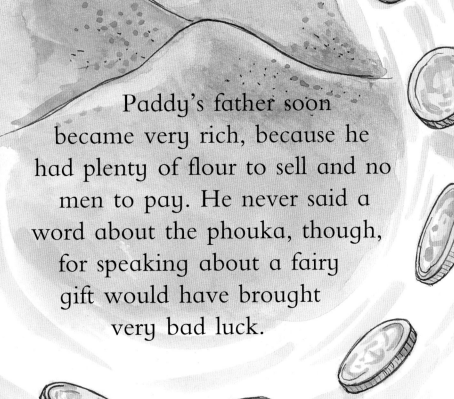

Paddy's father soon
became very rich, because he
had plenty of flour to sell and no
men to pay. He never said a
word about the phouka, though,
for speaking about a fairy
gift would have brought
very bad luck.

Paddy often hid in the chest to watch the phoukas. He felt sad that the old man, who worked so hard keeping the little ones in order and making them work, only had tattered rags to wear.

So he saved up his pocket money until he had enough to buy a very splendid suit of clothes which would keep the old phouka warm in the cold mill.

One night, before climbing into the old chest, he laid the clothes on the floor where the phouka usually stood.

When the old fairy came in, he saw the garments and was amazed. 'What's this? Are these for me?' he asked. 'I shall be a fine gentleman.'

The phouka put the suit on — there was even a silk waistcoat! — and paraded about in it. Then he looked at the corn, waiting to be ground. 'No more work for me!' he cried. 'I'm a gentleman now, and too grand to grind corn. I'm going on my travels!' He kicked his old rags into the corner, and disappeared into the darkness.

No corn was ground
that night – or ever
again, because all the
little phoukas ran
away. But Paddy's
father had made
enough money to keep
his family in comfort –
and when Paddy himself
got married, some years later,
a gorgeous gold cup, full of wine,
appeared at his place on the table.
Paddy knew the cup was a present
from the phouka, and his family
kept it as a treasure ever after.

Edited by Sheila Mortimer
Designed by Alyssa Peacock

Published by Gill & Macmillan Ltd
Hume Avenue, Park West, Dublin 12
with associated companies throughout the world
www.gillmacmillan.ie

ISBN 978 07171 4604 8
This edition produced by
Tony Potter Publishing Ltd, RH17 5PA
Copyright © 2008 Tony Potter Publishing Ltd
www.tonypotter.com

Printed in China

1 3 5 7 9 10 8 6 4 2